LITTLE SOUP'S HAYRIDE

D0709152

OTHER YOUNG YEARLING BOOKS
YOU WILL ENJOY

LITTLE SOUP'S BUNNY, *Robert Newton Peck*
LITTLE SOUP'S TURKEY, *Robert Newton Peck*
LITTLE SOUP'S BIRTHDAY, *Robert Newton Peck*
THE MYSTERY OF THE BLUE RING, *Patricia Reilly Giff*
THE RIDDLE OF THE RED PURSE,
Patricia Reilly Giff
THE SECRET AT THE POLK STREET SCHOOL,
Patricia Reilly Giff
THE POWDER PUFF PUZZLE, *Patricia Reilly Giff*
SOMETHING QUEER IS GOING ON, *Elizabeth Levy*
WRITE UP A STORM WITH THE POLK STREET SCHOOL,
Patricia Reilly Giff
COUNT YOUR MONEY WITH THE POLK STREET SCHOOL,
Patricia Reilly Giff

YEARLING BOOKS/YOUNG YEARLINGS/YEARLING CLASSICS
are designed especially to entertain and enlighten young
people. Patricia Reilly Giff, consultant to this series, received her bachelor's degree from Marymount College
and a master's degree in history from St. John's University. She holds a Professional Diploma in Reading and a
Doctorate of Humane Letters from Hofstra University.
She was a teacher and reading consultant for many years,
and is the author of numerous books for young readers.

For a complete listing of all Yearling titles, write to
Dell Readers Service, P.O. Box 1045,
South Holland, IL 60473.

LITTLE
SOUP'S
HAYRIDE

Robert Newton Peck

Illustrated by Charles Robinson

A YOUNG YEARLING BOOK

Published by
Dell Publishing
a division of
Bantam Doubleday Dell Publishing Group, Inc.
1540 Broadway
New York, New York 10036

If you purchased this book without a cover you should be aware that this book is stolen property. It was reported as "unsold and destroyed" to the publisher and neither the author nor the publisher has received any payment for this "stripped book."

Text copyright © 1991 by Robert Newton Peck
Illustrations copyright © 1991 by Charles Robinson

All rights reserved. No part of this book may be reproduced or transmitted in any form or by any means, electronic or mechanical, including photocopying, recording, or by any information storage and retrieval system, without the written permission of the Publisher, except where permitted by law.

The trademark Yearling® is registered in the U.S. Patent and Trademark Office.

The trademark Dell® is registered in the U.S. Patent and Trademark Office.

ISBN: 0-440-40383-9

Printed in the United States of America

June 1991

10 9 8 7 6 5 4

CWO

LITTLE SOUP'S HAYRIDE

One

"Rob!"
Someone was yelling my name.

I was lying in the shade of a maple tree. Trying to play my harmonica through my nose.

If you do this enough, nobody ever borrows your harmonica.

* * *

"Hey, Rob."

Looking up the road, I saw Soup.

He was my best pal. His real name was Luther Wesley Vinson. But I never called him Luther. I called him Soup. And he called me Rob, which is short for my full name, Robert Newton Peck.

Soup arrived running, even though it was a hot summer day.

"Howdy," I said. "What's up?"

"Horses," panted Soup. "And big ones."

I sat up. "Where?"

"Up to our house. So let's go."

"Okay," I said, "as soon as I tell my mother where we're going."

* * *

We went to Soup's barn.

Soup and I both lived on farms in Vermont. We were next-farm neighbors.

"Here come the horses," he said.

Soup was right.

Along came two big horses. We ran to meet them. They were Clydesdales, with lots of hair above their hooves.

Clydesdale horses are very strong.

Two of them pulled a wagon piled high with hay.

Hay is long, dried grass.

It has seeds on one end.

Before the hay is cut, it's green, but then it dries to a golden tan.

Fresh hay smells nice.

It smells as if farmers want to save summer, for a long winter.

Two men came with the wagon.
Soup's father and uncle.
They let Soup and me ride way up high on the load of hay.
A hayride is fun. A pile of fun.
We sank into the hay, covered ourselves up, and giggled.
Hay is prickly in a gentle and funny way.
It tickles.

The two men unloaded all of the hay, inside Soup's haybarn.
They used big, long forks.
Pitchforks.

Then they left with the horses and the empty wagon.

"Rob," said Soup, "let's do it."

Two

I looked at Soup.
"Do what?" I asked him.
He smiled.
"*We'll* have a hayride of our own.
One that will go a lot faster."
"We don't have any horses," I said.

"No," said Soup, "we sure don't. But I know where there's a wagon. We ought to help with the haying too. Then we'll sort of be *men*."

Soup led the way.
I followed him.
He headed up the meadow hill.
It wasn't far.
Yet it was very steep. But it didn't really matter, because Soup and I were on our way to being grown-up men.
When we got to the hilltop, however, both of us were puffing.
Like horses.
I looked around.
All I saw were cows. Soup's cows, and they were a long way away.

"Soup, I don't see a wagon."

He winked. "I'll show you."

Soup headed toward a fence.

When we climbed over the fence, we came to a trash pile.

"It's a dump," said Soup. "People come up here to throw away old things they don't want."

"I don't want them either."

"Rob," he said, "there's a wagon up here. I saw it last week."

Soup became very busy.

He looked under a mattress, and behind two busted barrels.

"Ah," he said at last.

"You found it?"

"Right. I found it. Come see."

I climbed to where Soup stood high on a heap of trash.

He pointed.

"Well," he said, "here it is."

I looked.

It wasn't much to see.

Yet I had to admit, what Soup had found really was a wagon.

But not a hay wagon.

It was a little red coaster wagon.

I touched it, to brush away the dust.

On its side were faded white letters. RADIO PAL. One of its wheels felt loose.

"What do you think, Rob?"

I scratched a bug bite. "Well, it sure is a small wagon."

Soup nodded. "It needs pals, like us."

"But," I said, "a wagon this size won't hold a lot of hay."

Soup nodded his head, very slowly.

"Maybe," he said, "it will."

Three

___

Snap!

Soup snapped his fingers.

"Rob," he said, "I have an idea."

"What is it?"

"We'll need some long boards," he said.

We looked through the trash.

Each of us found some boards.

Soup found eleven.

I found seven.

"Rob," said Soup, "that makes eighteen."

"Will that be enough?"

He nodded. "Enough."

"Good."

"Now," he said, "all we do is stack our boards on RADIO PAL, and we're on our way."

We loaded the wagon.

Not with hay. With boards.

All eighteen.

"There," said Soup. "Now we're off to the hayfield for our load."

"What are the boards for?"

"Oh," said Soup, "you'll soon see."

I soon saw.

But it wasn't easy getting our wagon to the hayfield. The wagon had no handle.

We couldn't pull it like a team of horses.

So, we pushed it. Uphill.

We grunted all the way up.

I still didn't know what all those boards were for.

But then Soup explained, between grunts.

"We want a big load of hay," he said. "Not just a little bit."

I looked at our little red wagon.

RADIO PAL wasn't very big.

Its bin wouldn't hold very much hay.

Or very much boy.

At last we reached the hayfield.

"Here," said Soup, "is how we'll use our boards."

He placed the boards flat across the low sides of the wagon.

Soup made a large, flat bed of wood, so it looked like an empty hay wagon.

Then we hauled many armfuls of hay.

Hauled and hauled and hauled.

Four

"Wow," I said.

I looked at our wagon.

RADIO PAL was now out of sight.

All I could see was hay.

Lots of it.

Armful after armful. The long boards really helped hold a large load.

"Now, that," said Soup, "is a haystack. On wheels."

"And," I said, "it's all ours."

"So let's take it to the barn, just the way grown-up men do, with horses."

The load of hay was so tall and so wide that we couldn't see where we were pushing.

But we pushed.

We never touched the wagon.

Only the hay.

As we came to the top of a hill, below us, in the valley, lay Soup's farm. Just down the hill.

Both of us were wet with sweat.

Hayseeds stuck to me, all over.

Some were down my neck.

And itchy.

"Gosh," I said, "haying is hard work."

Soup was smiling.

"Rob, the hard part is over."

"That's right," I told him. "From here, the pushing will be easy."

"Wrong," he said.

"Wrong?"

Soup smiled. "We won't have to push."

"We won't?"

"No."

"How'll we get it there?"

Soup grinned. "We *ride.*"

Soup was right. From up here, it would be downhill, all the way to Soup's barn.

"But," he said, "we have to make sure of just one thing."

"What's that?"

"Point our wagon the right way."

I looked at our hayload.

"Soup, how will we steer?"

"Easy," he said. "We *lean.*"

Five

"Push," said Soup.
"I'm pushing."
"Then push harder."

Bracing my bare feet, I pushed harder.

It wasn't easy to push.

Soup was riding. That was easy.

Pushing was the hard part.

"I can't see," I said.

"That's okay, Rob. I can."

I was behind the wagon, pushing. Soup was up high on our load of hay.

He was sitting.

"Rob, keep pushing. Only an inch or so to go, and the wagon will roll all by itself."

I pushed an inch.

Then another.

Soup was right.

The pushing grew easier.

And easier.

Then the wagon kept going. By itself.

"Run," yelled Soup. "Come on."

I ran.

Ahead of me, the wagon also seemed to be in a bit of a hurry.

But I ran faster.

I caught up. And jumped on.

"Wow," I said, "that was close."

"See," said Soup, who was seated in the pile of hay beside me, "we're rolling, Rob."

I brushed hayseeds from my eyes.

"Right toward the barn," I said.

The meadow hill wasn't very steep. Not at first. But then I could see ahead.

We rolled faster.

Our wagon picked up speed.

Below us, under the hay, the boards rattled on the metal lips of the wagon bin.

Somewhere, under us, was RADIO PAL.

But all I saw was hay.

Faster we rolled.

And faster!

"Soup," I said, blinking the hayseeds from my eyes, "we're not pointed toward the barn."

"No," said Soup, "not quite yet."

"What'll we do?"

"Lean!"

We leaned.

Yet nothing happened.

No, that's wrong. Something did happen.

The wagon rolled even faster.

Six

"Lean," shouted Soup again.
"I'm leaning. I'm leaning!"

I was leaning so far to my right that I nearly fell off the wagon.

RADIO PAL seemed to be going nuts.

Our little wagon, with its giant load of hay, wanted to go somewhere or other.

Where?

I couldn't tell.

When I ride fast, my eyes water.

Right now, they were dripping like a pair of April icicles.

I wiped my eyes in a hurry.

Then I saw.

Too late.

"Soup," I yelled, "we're heading for . . ."

"Don't say it, Rob. I know."

I didn't say it.

I saw it.

Faster and faster, we rolled.

I thought riding would be fun.

Maybe I was wrong.

Perhaps it wouldn't be as much fun as I had hoped.

At first, our ride was slow.

But it wasn't slow anymore.

As the hill became steeper, our hayride became a lot faster.

"Soup," I said, "will we fall off?"

"If we're lucky," he yelled.

I didn't know that the hill in Soup's cow meadow was so steep.

I didn't know it was so long.

Or . . . so bumpy.

Bump.

Bump, bump.

Bump, bump, bump.

Bump, bump, bump, bump.

Bump, bump, bump, bump, bump.

That's how steep the hill really was.

"Hang on," Soup was yelling.

"There's nothing to hang on to."

There wasn't.

So, we did the next best thing.

We hung on to each other.

And screamed.

RADIO PAL did not scream.

It just bounced. And rattled.

Faster and faster and faster.

"Rob," said Soup, in almost a whisper, "there's bad news."

"How bad?"

"Very."

"What is it?"

"I'm afraid we're going to do it."
"Do *what*?" I asked Soup.

He answered in a word.

"Crash."

Seven

"Help," I wanted to yelp.
"It's no use, Rob."
"We're really going to crash?"

"Yes," said Soup, "and not into the barn."

I looked.

I was looking straight ahead, and down the steep hill.

My eyes were not seeing too clearly.

What I saw was foggy.

But I did see what was ahead, and it was too terrible to think about.

"Oh, no," I yelled.

"Do you see it?" Soup hollered.

"I see it."

"It's dead ahead."

"And full of smelly mud."

"Yuk."

I leaned.

So did Soup.

Bump, bump, bump, bump.

It didn't do any good.

No good at all.

Because, dead ahead, there was a very small pigpen, next to a very large barn.

I wanted to close my eyes, but they wouldn't close.

And my mouth wouldn't shut.

Hayseeds were flying up, and into my open mouth. It made me feel like a cow.

Ahead, the pigpen began to grow.

Larger and larger.

I was remembering last summer.

Something awful happened to me.

Do you want to know what it was?

Okay, I'll tell you.

I was trying to walk on a fence rail.

The rail was on the pig fence.

There was mud on my feet, and also in between my toes.

Slippery mud.

I fell into the pigpen, and it smelled a lot worse than mud.

"Soup . . ."

"What is it?"

"Maybe we ought to jump."

"Jump off?"

"Yes."

"*No.*"

"Why not?"

"We're going too fast."

"How fast are we going?" I asked.

"About a hundred miles an hour."

"Is that all?"

"Maybe even two hundred."

"Yowie."

Closing my eyes, I was getting ready to do only one thing.

Die.

Eight

I prayed.
Soup screamed.
RADIO PAL did something too.

It rattled its boards, spilled a little hay, and then did something far worse.

I saw it.

"Soup," I yelled.

"What is it?"

"Something's wrong with our wagon. RADIO PAL just lost a part."

"Which part?"

"A wheel."

There was a pause. A short one.

"Oh, no," Soup groaned.

Now, I was thinking, we couldn't lean to the left. Or to the right.

As we rolled down the hill, I saw something racing beside us.

I couldn't believe what I saw.

But there it was.

Racing us.

It was small, round, and black . . . with a circle of red on it.

"Soup . . ."

"What is it?"

"Look . . . beside us."

He looked.

Then he said what I already knew.

"Rob, it's our wheel. And it's on your side."

"I know."

"So . . . do it."

"Do what?"

"Grab our wheel," said Soup.

"Now?"

"Yes," screamed Soup. "Right now."

"I'll fall off."

"No you won't, Rob. I'll hold you."

Maybe our only chance was to get

our wheel back on good old RADIO PAL.

"Okay," I said, "here goes. Hang on to my pants."

"Right," said Soup. "Go get it."

I stretched out my arm.

My fingers were not even close, so I leaned out and away from the racing wagon.

I could feel Soup's knuckles against my backbone. He was grabbing the belt of my pants.

"Hold on to me, Soup."

"I will."

"Don't let go."

"I won't," said Soup.

"Promise?"

"Yes, I promise."

"Cross your heart?"

Soup's finger made a quick X.

"Cross my heart," said Soup, "and hope to die."

"Don't say *that.*"

Nine

Bump.
The little wheel hit a bump.
Up it hopped.

I tried to grab it, and missed.

Soup was pulling on the belt that was around the waist of my pants.

The wheel flew high into the air.

I stood up, trying to grab it, high above my head.

Then it fell.

My fingers opened like a claw.

Would I be able to catch it?

I could catch a baseball.

But a wheel might be a lot harder.

I saw it spinning in the air.

My hands reached out and caught the wheel.

"I got it."

But then a thought hit me.

What was I going to do with it?

There was no way to reach the axle, because of all that hay.

"What'll I do with the wheel?"

"*Steer,*" yelled Soup.

"What? Are you crazy?"

"Rob, pretend it's a steering wheel. And hurry. We're going to crash."

Pretending to steer, I held the loose wheel in front of me.

I held it with both hands.

"It's not helping," I said.

"It's not hurting," said Soup. "Keep steering."

RADIO PAL hit another bump.

A big rock.

It changed our direction.

"We're pointing toward my house," said Soup.

Ahead of us, I saw somebody I knew.

It was Soup Vinson's mother.

She stood at her clothesline.

Mrs. Vinson was hanging wet clothes outside to dry in the sun.

Closer and closer we rolled.

RADIO PAL had only three wheels, but it still rolled faster than four.

Mrs. Vinson turned around.

She saw us coming.

She screamed. Her hands covered her mouth, but she still screamed, and her eyes became very large.

"Stop," she hollered at us.

"We can't," Soup hollered back.

"We're going too fast," I yelled.

In the next five seconds, things happened, one right after another.

All of them were bad.

Ten

We hit the clean wash.
Not the sheets. Not the shirts.

Some of it seemed to be underwear.
But not for men.
It was pink with white lace.

* * *

Soup's mother screamed again.
Then fainted.
Our wagon did not stop.
"Lean," said Soup.
I leaned.
So did Soup.
He still held on to my pants.
It felt as though my belt was breaking. But my belt wouldn't break.
It was strong and made of cowhide.
Old cowhide.

It broke.
Pop!
RADIO PAL hit another bump.
We flew up into the air.

I couldn't see where. Because hay seemed to be flying all over.

It's hard to see with wet pink underwear wrapped around your head.

As I flew through the air, something else happened.

Soup yanked.

My pants pulled loose.

Off they slid.

I wasn't wearing any underwear of my own that day, but at least I had Mrs. Vinson's.

It was no time to be fussy.

When you're flying through the air with no pants on, it's hard to do what I did.

It's very hard to do.

How I did it I'll never know.

But in one second, I did it.

I put on Mrs. Vinson's underwear while doing a triple flip.

At the end of the third flip, something worse happened.

We landed.

In the pigpen.

Ker-splatt.

The pig squealed a dirty word. "Oink."

Soup's mother said a word too.

It wasn't "oink." Soup and I were now knee-deep in soft brown mud. Hay and laundry were floating slowly to the ground.

* * *

Soup's mother came running our way, as the pig ran around us in circles, inside the square pigpen.

Mrs. Vinson did the same thing, in circles, only outside the pen. Neither of them ran in squares. Yet both of them were squealing.

Mrs. Vinson stopped and stared at me. "Robert," she told me, "take off my underwear."

"Yes'm," I said.

Mrs. Vinson turned her back.

I took it off. It didn't matter.

I was wearing lots of mud.

Soup was laughing.

"Rob," he said, *"we're not dead."*

"No," I said. "And neither is the pig."

Looking around, I saw our little wagon.

RADIO PAL lay upside down, in mud and hay and laundry, its three wheels still spinning.

I was holding the fourth.

Wooden boards lay everywhere.

Soup sat in the mud. He was still laughing, and holding on to my pants.

"Here," he said. "Put 'em on."

Have you ever tried to put on muddy pants when you are knee-deep in pig mud?

Soup and I both giggled, because we were so very dirty.

And so very alive.

"Ha, ha, ha," I laughed.

"Ho, ho, ho," laughed Soup.

Radio Pal said nothing, but I knew our wagon felt happy, like Soup and me. Nothing's more fun than getting dirty.

"Oink," said the pig.

But Soup's mother wasn't laughing.

Her face wore a very stern look.

Right then, I knew that Soup and I were going to *get it*.

We would get something that both of us didn't like, and we were going to *get it* right now. What every kid hates to get. Something terrible.

Painful. Awful. And all over.

Too horrible to describe.

Soup's mother was going to give one to each of us.

A bath.